Once, long ago, a race of robot beings called Autobots were forced to wage war against another race of robots called Decepticons, to bring peace back to their home planet of Cybertron. As the war went on, chance brought both sides to Earth. They crashed so violently on landing that all the robots lay in the Earth's crust, seemingly without life, for over four million years.

Suddenly the energy set in motion by a powerful volcanic eruption gives them life once more – and the war starts all over again here on Earth. Among the robots' many strange powers is the ability to transform into other shapes, and they use this to disguise themselves to fit in with the civilisation they find on Earth. The Autobots have to defend themselves and they have to protect this planet with all its valuable resources and the people who live here.

Leaders come and go. Galvatron travels back from the 21st century to take over from Megatron, commander of the Decepticons. Then the strange disappearance of Optimus Prime leaves the Autobots without a leader, and Ultra Magnus arrives from Cybertron to take his place, as the Autobots' new commander.

And so the fight goes on – both now and far into the future, on different time levels.

British Library Cataloguing in Publication Data

Grant, John, 1930-
    Galvatron's Air Attack.—(Transformers)
    I. Title II. Dunn, Richard III. Series
    823'.914[J]   PZ7
    ISBN 0-7214-0988-1

First edition

Published by Ladybird Books Ltd Loughborough Leicestershire UK
Ladybird Books Inc Lewiston Maine 04240 USA

THE TRANSFORMERS™

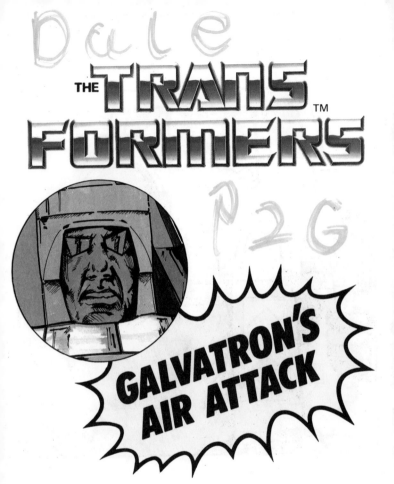

GALVATRON'S AIR ATTACK

written by JOHN GRANT
illustrated by RICHARD DUNN

Ladybird Books

In the surgical repair shop of Metroplex, the Autobot city of Earth, Ratchet was hard at work. Several Autobots had been damaged in fighting with the Decepticons. Most were suffering from knocks and scrapes. Hot Rod had a bad dent in one side, and a buckled wheel.

"Come on! Come on!" he cried, impatiently, as Ratchet and Wheeljack looked at the damage. "It isn't all that bad! A couple of taps with a hammer and I'll be up and out of here!"

Ratchet shook his head. "It isn't that easy. I can fix that wheel so that you can get about. But it will soon have to be replaced with a new one."

"I could make a replacement easily," said Wheeljack. "That is, if I could get the materials. Earth metals are not bad, but we really need cybernite. And there's almost none left among our stores."

Later that day, Ratchet reported to Ultra Magnus. "Unless we can get hold of the special metals, like cybernite, that I need to do repairs, many of the Autobots will no longer be able to function."

Ultra Magnus looked serious. "The only place we can find such things is back on our home planet, Cybertron. And we do not yet have the resources to fight off the Decepticons and return there to look for it."

Kup had been listening to the conversation. "There *is* a way to get supplies of those special

materials," he said, "without leaving Earth. We have fought many battles with the Decepticons since we arrived here. Some of the bigger fights left many Autobots and Decepticons wrecked and lost. I remember, when I was a young Autobot, a great battle which raged from dawn till dusk in a mountain valley. I don't recall who won, but I do remember that the valley was strewn with wreckage afterwards. If the Decepticons haven't got there first, we might find what we need. If I can find the valley again!"

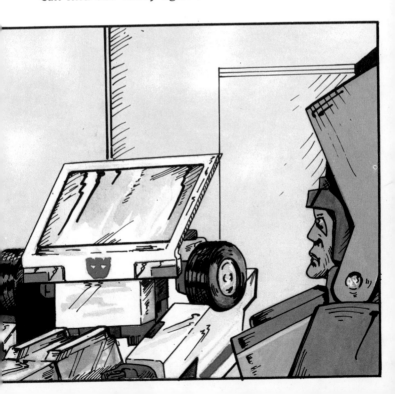

While Kup went off to look at some maps and try to refresh his memory, Ultra Magnus set about organising a salvage expedition to visit the old battlefield and collect everything they could that might be useful.

Soon the Autobot convoy was ready to roll. Kup was to lead the way: he was sure that he could find the place. Next came Wheeljack. His job would be to choose the most useful bits and pieces. Hoist and Grapple made up the rest of the party. They would lift and drag any bigger pieces of wreckage they might find.

There was a sound of running footsteps. It was Spike, the young Earth friend of the Autobots. He stopped, panting, in front of Ultra Magnus, and looked up at the giant figure towering above him.

"Please," he cried, "can I go too? I could be very useful. Earth people know a lot that even Autobots don't!"

Ultra Magnus laughed. "All right, Spike," he said. "Just don't get in the way."

"Thanks!" cried Spike. Then he ran across to Kup and climbed into the cab as the engines roared and the Autobots moved out.

To avoid being seen, the Autobots left their city at dusk. Night was falling as they raced along deserted roads towards the mountains and the valley where the battle had been fought so long ago.

Suddenly, the northern sky was lit up by brilliant flashes of light. The flashes became streamers which rippled and glowed against the dark sky.

The Autobots halted. "Take cover!" cried Kup. "Decepticons!"

Spike laughed. "That's not the Decepticons," he said. "That's the northern lights: the aurora borealis. It won't hurt us."

"What causes it?" asked Kup.

"I've been told that it's some sort of electricity in the upper atmosphere," said Spike. "It sometimes interferes with radio communications."

In the light of a full moon, the Autobots reached the valley. They transformed out of their vehicle shapes and stood waiting as Kup walked along the valley floor, examining the landscape.

He rejoined the others. "Yes, it's just as I remember. Those were the days. We took up our positions along the hillside, there. The Decepticons tried to get behind us over on that hill. One of them was a real giant. I forget what they called him now. There we were! Face to face! It was me or him! And then, suddenly...!"

But Grapple interrupted. "Tell us all about it another time, Old Timer. We're here to work, not to listen to accounts of your heroic past."

The Autobots scattered across the valley, their sensors tuned to find cybernite and other extra-terrestrial metals.

Spike climbed a little way up the hill and found a sheltered ledge. There he sat and searched in the moonlight for a sign of smashed machines and wrecked robots from the ancient battle.

Spike strained his eyes to see in the half-light.
Below him the Autobots crossed and recrossed
the valley, searching every crack and hollow. As
Spike listened to the clanking sound of their metal
footsteps, he suddenly heard something else. A
distant whine rose to a scream, and then to a
roar. Like evil birds, a flight of jet aircraft swept
over the hills, weapons firing.

The Autobots raced for cover. Then one by
one the planes came in to land. Immediately, each
transformed into a heavily armed robot.

"Decepticons!" cried Spike.

From the cover of rocks and boulders, the Autobots kept up a steady fire against the enemy, forcing them to withdraw for a moment.

Then Spike saw the Autobots transform again into their vehicle shapes and race at top speed for the entrance to the valley. Keeping in the shadows, he ran to meet them.

Kup slowed as he saw Spike at the edge of the track. Spike threw himself into the back, and the car accelerated with the others into a narrow gorge leading out of the valley.

As the Autobots beat a retreat, the Decepticons also transformed, and followed them. Jets roaring, Starscream led Thrust, Cyclonus, Scourge and Dirge low and fast in pursuit. The Autobots disappeared into the shadows of the gorge.

Almost at the last moment the Decepticons saw that the gorge was too narrow for their wingspans. They banked sharply between the

rocky walls. Dirge misjudged the distance, and his wing-tip showered sparks as it struck rock. Climbing vertically with pieces dropping from the damaged wing, Dirge flew clear of the gorge and back to a bumpy landing on the valley floor.

Where the gorge was narrowest, the Autobots transformed again to robots. As the flying Decepticons tried to reach them they came under fierce fire from laser weapons.

At length they gave up, and the sound of their engines faded in the distance. Last to go was Dirge, wobbling into the air with the last shots of the Autobots whizzing around him.

Dawn was breaking as the Autobots arrived back at Metroplex. Ultra Magnus listened to Kúp's report.

"We didn't find anything," said the wise old Autobot. "But we might have done if we had not been ambushed by the Decepticons. What puzzles me is... how did they know that we were coming? There has been no Decepticon activity reported from that quarter for a long time. I checked before we left. And we saw no signs of

them on the way on any of our detection systems."

"They must have found some new way of keeping us under surveillance," said Ultra Magnus. "Perhaps they have an outpost in the hills that we know nothing of."

Silverbolt spoke. "I suggest that we carry out a thorough examination of the whole area of the old battlefield. I can be ready for take-off at first light tomorrow."

"Very well," agreed Ultra Magnus.

Meanwhile, at the Decepticon base, Galvatron watched the return of Starscream, Thrust, Scourge and Cyclonus. Dirge came in to land just behind them, barely in full control. The damaged Decepticon bounced heavily on the runway and slid to a halt close to Galvatron. As the Decepticons transformed to robots, Galvatron cried, "The surveillance system? It worked?"

"Perfectly," said Cyclonus. "They had no warning until we were on them."

"So they were destroyed?" asked the Decepticon leader.

"Well, no," replied Cyclonus. "They took refuge in a rocky canyon. We couldn't..."

"You couldn't deal with a bunch of simple-minded idiots like the Autobots!" interrupted Galvatron. "And what happened to *him*?" he said, looking at Dirge.

"I accidentally hit the rocks," said Dirge, apologetically.

"Go and get the damage seen to!" snapped Galvatron. "And I suggest that you take some flying lessons! You haven't heard the last of this!"

As the sun rose, the Aerialbots led by Silverbolt flew into the sky above Metroplex and set course for the hills around the old battle-field.

As the place came in view, Silverbolt flew low. Then with a scream of jets, Slingshot, Skydive, Fireflight and Air Raid zoomed off to scout the land below. Immediately, Silverbolt climbed high into the morning sky, watching the smaller craft skimming the hills beneath him.

By midday the scouts had examined every inch
of the country for a place where the Decepticons
could have placed a spy installation. But they
found nothing. They signalled to Silverbolt, and
the large plane was about to descend to them
when its video-radar sensors gave a brief flicker.
It had picked up something. Silverbolt dived
quickly, and the smaller aircraft attached
themselves to him to create the mighty Superion.

At full power, Superion rose up and up to the
last fringes of the Earth's atmosphere and the edge
of space itself. This time, there was no doubting
it. Something big but invisible was being picked
up by the radar.

Galvatron stood with Soundwave in the main control complex of the Decepticon base. On a video display screen a small dot moved slowly.

"What is it?" asked Galvatron.

"AUTOBOT PATROL...HIGH ALTITUDE AIRCRAFT...DESCENDING NOW...
...CONTACT FADING."

"Why didn't you have it destroyed?" cried Galvatron.

"HOSTILE ACTION WOULD REVEAL SURVEILLANCE SATELLITE...IN TEN HOURS REFRACTION SHIELD WILL BE OPERATING."

"Good!" cried Galvatron. "The three surveillance space stations keep all parts of the planet in view at all times. We can see every move made by the enemy, no matter how well he thinks he is hidden. And the refraction shields will make the stations totally invisible."

High above Earth, on the edge of space,
Decepticon Space Station Argon orbited slowly.
The Station Commander, Blitzwing, watched his
crew as they adjusted the controls that kept the
giant satellite in position.

Suddenly, lights flashed on the control panel,
and the voice of Soundwave came through the
audio system.

"STAND BY FOR REFRACTION SHIELD
ACTIVATION...FIVE...FOUR... ...THREE...
TWO...ONE...ACTIVATING."

For a moment, the Decepticons who were watching through the viewing ports saw a flicker of blue light run along the metal structure of the space station. Soundwave's voice sounded again.

"ACTIVATION COMPLETE...ALL STATIONS NOW INVISIBLE TO EXTERNAL SENSORS."

Blitzwing spoke into the radio, "Acknowledge." He turned to the Decepticon crew. "Now we can spy on the Autobots without their ever guessing where we are."

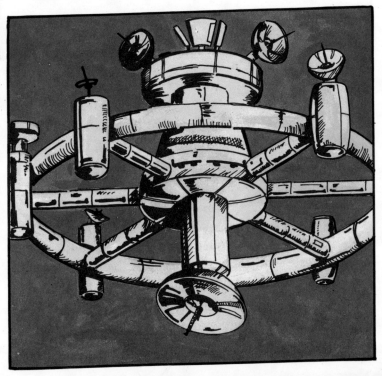

Ultra Magnus studied the recordings of Superion's radar contact.

"I think that we have found at least part of the answer," he said. "There *is* something up there. Some device which enables the Decepticons to keep watch on us at all times."

"A spy-in-the-sky satellite?" asked Spike.

"No, something much bigger," said the Autobot leader. "But out of visual range. Someone must investigate who can go farther than the Aerialbots. Tell Cosmos that I have a task for him."

A short time later, Silverbolt took off again. Tucked into his cargo compartment was the small

saucer spy Autobot, Cosmos. At maximum
altitude, Silverbolt said, "It's all yours, Cosmos.
Good luck." And the small saucer dropped clear
of the plane, hovered for a moment, then sped up
and out into the blackness of space.

Within seconds, Cosmos picked up a radio
signal on the Decepticon wavelength. Then
another. And another. He circled high above
Earth. There was nothing to be seen, but there
was a continuous flow of radio messages. Some
were from Decepticon headquarters, but the
others were from space. Cosmos recorded
everything, then headed back to Metroplex with
all speed.

Ultra Magnus heard Cosmos' report, then Hound analysed the recordings of the Decepticon radio messages.

"You were right," he said to Ultra Magnus. "This is no ordinary spy-in-the-sky. We're talking now about full-scale orbiting space stations – three of them. They are so carefully positioned that there is no part of the Earth's surface which escapes the eyes of the Decepticons. They must have some sort of shielding system that makes them impossible to see."

"They must be destroyed," said Ultra Magnus.

"That will be difficult, if not impossible," said Hound. "We do not have the capability for a frontal attack in space."

"I remember, in the Battle of the Green Asteroid," put in Kup, "the enemy was out of range. We put out false signals to lure him closer."

"We could give it a try," said the Autobot leader.

"I have an idea," said Spike.

"When I was a little boy," said Spike, "my dad used to tell me stories. One of my favourites was about a little man who had two fierce enemies. They were giants, and he was helpless to do anything. But he tricked the giants into thinking that each had attacked the other, and as a result, they destroyed each other. Couldn't we do something the same with the three space stations?"

Kup laughed. "I don't think that we could trick

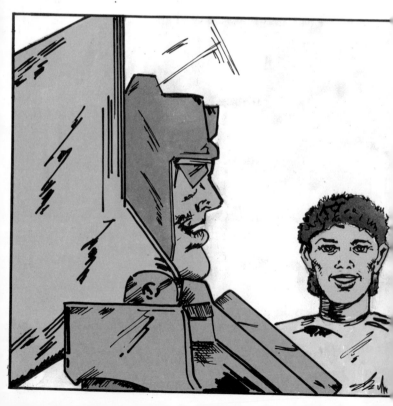

the Decepticons into fighting each other. But, Spike, you've given me an idea. Perhaps they can be made to destroy their own space stations. Stick around. We'll need your help. You're almost as smart as an Autobot!"

"What's your plan, Kup?" asked Ultra Magnus.

"Give me some time to think it out more," was the answer. "It's going to take a lot of hard work and ingenuity."

Kup went to look for Huffer and Wheeljack. When he found them, he had a long discussion with them. Then, he sent for Spike.

"Tell us more about the northern lights," he said. "Is it true that they interfere with radio transmissions?"

"That's what I've heard my dad say," replied Spike. "When there's a display of northern lights in the sky, you can hardly hear anything on the radio for static."

"Good," said Kup. "Now I know what we are going to do. Huffer and Wheeljack say that they can build a transmitter which will trigger off a display of the northern lights in the upper atmosphere. That will blot out radio signals between the Decepticon space stations, and between them and their base. Hound can send false messages which will get through the static. The Decepticons will not know whether they are coming or going. It should be fun! For us!"

They reported their plan to Ultra Magnus. It would take time to set up, Wheeljack told the leader. They would need the help of every Autobot who could be spared from other duties.

Work started immediately.

Ten days later the work was complete. Power-generating and amplifying equipment was loaded aboard Ultra Magnus and driven to an isolated mountain top. Grapple followed behind to do the heavy lifting.

The two normal-looking vehicles parked quietly until after dark. Then Spike and a swarm of the smaller Autobots began unloading the gear.

Spike looked up at the dark sky. "The Decepticons are bound to spot us," he said.

"Yes," said Swerve. "We have to move fast, and hit them before they can decide what to do."

Swiftly the apparatus was assembled. From a small pack, a thing like a gigantic umbrella opened out. It was a radio aerial. But it would not transmit messages. It was designed to send a megavolt charge of electricity into the sky. Kup hoped that it would work, and that a display of northern lights would be triggered off such as no one had ever seen before.

Kup threw a switch. There was a crackle and a loud humming from the equipment. Then first the horizon, and then the whole sky, was lit up with the flash and flicker of the Autobots' own aurora borealis!

Aboard Decepticon Space Station Argon, Station Commander Blitzwing stared at the communication panel. The last message from base had been suddenly drowned out by a roar of static. The radio Decepticon adjusted the controls. But the message was gone.

Then, through the static came a familiar sound. The voice of Soundwave.

"EMERGENCY...SPACE STATION ARGON ...RE-DEPLOY TO CO-ORDINATES ALPHA – 9 – 0 – 2...IMMEDIATE!"

Blitzwing turned and shouted orders. The rocket motors on the outer rim of the space station flamed into life. Slowly at first, but gathering speed to hyper-sonic velocity, Space Station Argon headed for its new location.

At the same time, Space Stations Krypton and Xenon were also being re-deployed – to the same location: co-ordinates alpha – 9 – 0 – 2.

Far below, Kup looked up. "All we do now is wait," he said. "Hound's imitation of Soundwave could have fooled me. Let's hope that it fooled the Decepticons."

At the Decepticon base, Galvatron screamed as he watched the video display screen. "What are those lunatics doing?" he raged.

Near the centre of the screen, three blips moved rapidly towards each other. "They've gone mad! Tell them to stop and get back on station."

"NO COMMUNICATION...ABNORMAL STATIC!" said Soundwave.

"Can't they see what's going to happen? They're on collision course!" cried Galvatron.

"They're invisible to each other!" cried
Starscream.

Galvatron lunged across the control panel and
threw the switch which de-activated the refraction
shield. But...too late! On the screen, the three
dots came together and disappeared!

On the ground, Spike and the Autobots saw a
distant flash in the sky as the Decepticon space
stations collided and smashed into a thousand
pieces.

Ultra Magnus was waiting to congratulate the party on their return to Metroplex. "That was a super team effort," he said. "It is only by team-work that we will eventually win victory over the Decepticons."

He looked around. "Where are Kup and Wheeljack?"

At that moment the two rolled up and transformed. "That was a job well done," said Ultra Magnus.